North-South Books

New York

My Magic Cloth

A STORY FOR A WHOLE WEEK

Written and Illustrated by
HEIDE HELENE BEISERT
Retold by
NAOMI LEWIS

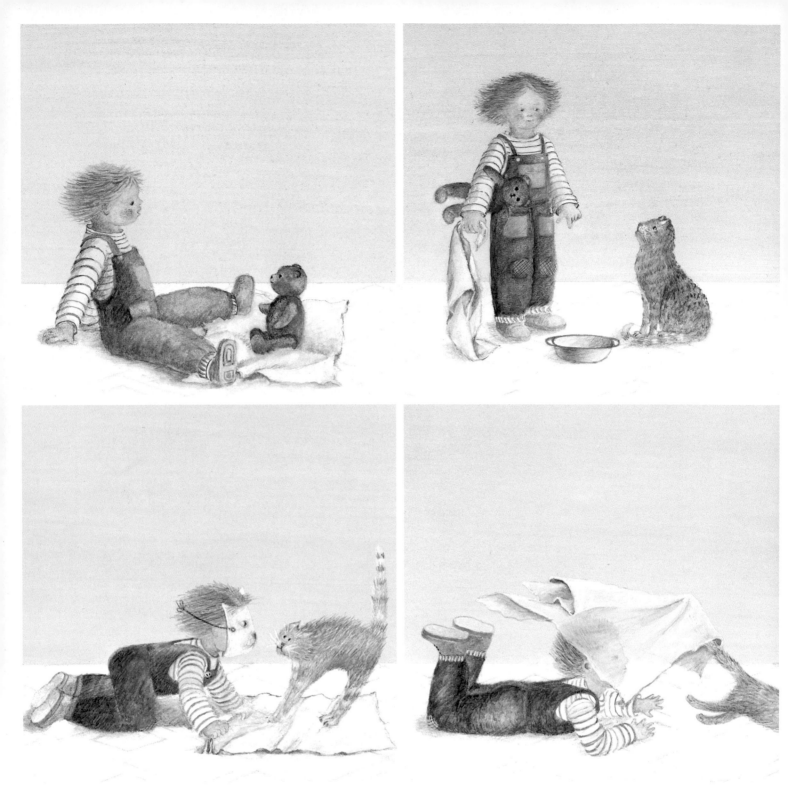

"It's Monday," said Teddy, the little bear. "What are we going
to do today?"
"Today?" said Tom. "Today I'm going to be a lion." He waved his special
magic cloth; the one he took with him everywhere, even to bed.
"Yes," he told the cat, "I shall ROAR! I shall eat you up!"
"Oh no, you won't," said Puss. And off he ran.

Evening came. Tom and Teddy were asleep in bed.
But Puss was not; he slipped out of the window and vanished.
Then a mighty lion appeared in the distance.
He came nearer and nearer: pad, pad, pad.

"Wake up, Thomas!" roared the lion. "I'm coming for you!"
"Oh no," said Tom. "I am going to catch you with my magic cloth."
And he ran barefoot over the hot desert sand.

Soon Tom caught the splendid lion, and he climbed with Teddy onto his golden back. "Now take us home," said Tom. "And you go to bed as well, you naughty lion."

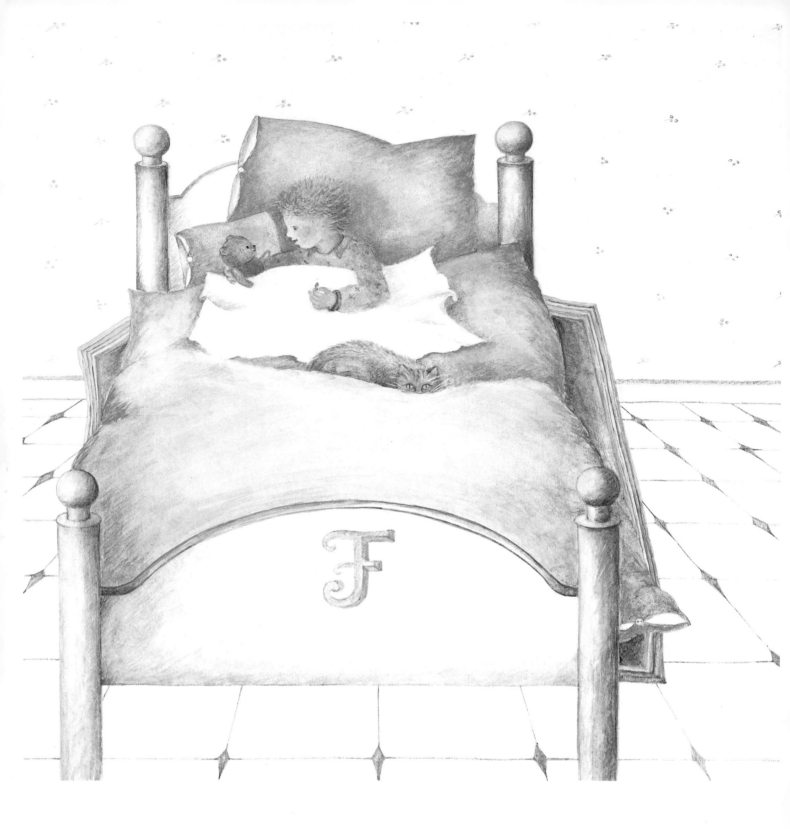

"Tuesday!" said Tom next morning. "It's a good day
for climbing beanstalks. But first we must plant some beans."
"Yes, let's do that," said Teddy. "They always grow quickly
in fairy tales."

They found some flowerpots, filled them with earth and
planted the beans. Then they waited.
Nothing happened.
By night time Teddy was very sad. "They don't want to grow," he said.
But Tom had another idea. "They need some sleep to help them grow,"
he said. "I'll cover them with my cloth."

In the night the beans... began... to... grow...

They looked like a lovely waving forest.
They settled Tom and Teddy in the magic cloth
and rocked them tenderly as they slept.

The next morning Tom went to fetch his cloth from the flowerpots.
He called to Teddy, "Quick! Come and look at the beans!"

"No, you come here," said Teddy. "It's Wednesday. Yesterday was for beans; today is for butterflies. Look! The garden is full of them."

"I didn't catch a single one," said Tom that evening.

"Never mind about chasing them," said a voice.
It came from the magic cloth!
"We three are going to fly through the air, just like butterflies."
They floated out into the pale blue-violet sky.

"It's Thursday," said Teddy. "May we play something special?"
"No playing today," said Tom severely. "It's wash day."

"I hate Thursdays," grumbled Teddy. But at last the work was done.
They watched the washing dancing on the line.

"It's Friday," announced Tom. "Let's do something different."
"Shall we visit the bees?" asked Teddy. "They might give us
some honey."

But the bees were not pleased to see them. "We work hard to make the honey. Why should you take it?" they cried. "Go away."

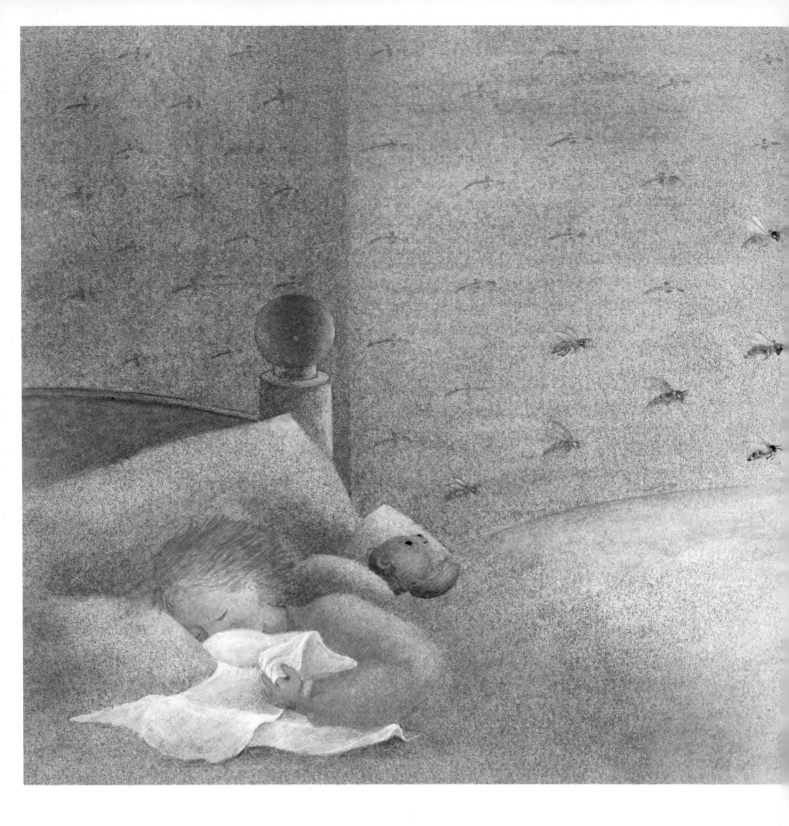

"What nasty bees!" complained Teddy.
"One of them has stung my finger, too," said Tom.
But when he wrapped his special cloth around it, all the hurt went away.
His finger was well again.

And listen to this!
While the two were asleep, the bees flew gently back.
"Cheer up!" they said. "We are bringing you some honey,
honey for Tom and his bear."

Tom felt happy when he woke. "I know why!" he shouted. "It's Saturday
– the best day of all for play. Pay attention, Teddy.
       I am the wizard Hokus!
       I work a hocus pocus.
       With my magic, one, two, three,
       You shall grow as big as me."

In the evening Tom looked at his bear. "You are still very small," he said.
"Don't worry," answered Teddy. "Just wait a little longer."

And he was right! Never forget the magic cloth!
In the night, Teddy grew bigger... and bigger... and bigger.

What a fine large handsome bear he had become!
He took Tom in his arms and carried him far, far, far away,
through ice and snow, over the mountains, to the kingdom of the bears.

It was a bright clear Sunday morning.
"Tom, where are you?" called his mother.
She opened the door of his room.

The magic cloth stirred in the breeze from the open window.
"Sh-h-h," it whispered. "He is still asleep."

Copyright © 1986 by Nord-Süd Verlag, Mönchaltorf, Switzerland.
First published in Switzerland under the title *Das Schnuffeltuch*.
English translation copyright © 1986 by Naomi Lewis.
North-South Books English language edition copyright © 1986 by
Rada Matija AG, 8625 Gossau ZH, Switzerland.

10   9   8   7   6   5   4   3   2

First published in the United States, Great Britain, Canada, Australia and
New Zealand in 1986 by North-South Books, an imprint of Rada Matija AG.

Library of Congress Catalog Card Number: 86-60490.

British Library Cataloguing in Publication Data

Beisert, Heide Helene
   My magic cloth.
   I. Title   II. Das Schnuffeltuch. *English*
   833'.914[J]   PZ7

ISBN 1-55858-069-7